Summer

A Level Two Reader

By Cynthia Klingel and Robert B. Noyed

The
Child's
World®

2

Summer is here! Summer is a season. It comes after spring and before fall.

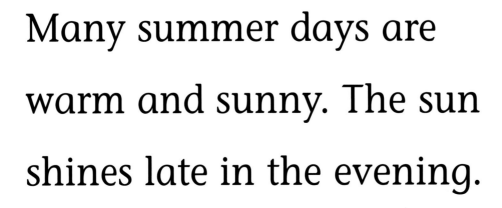

Many summer days are warm and sunny. The sun shines late in the evening.

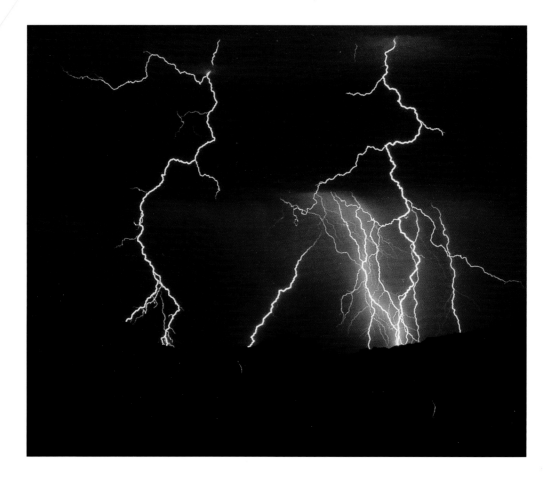

Sometimes there are strong storms. There can be thunder, lightning, and heavy rain. Some storms may cause tornadoes.

The rain and hot sun make plants grow. The trees are full of leaves.

Many people have gardens in the summer. They grow tomatoes, beans, peas, and carrots. Strawberries, raspberries, and blueberries are ready for picking.

Bees are very busy in the summer. They buzz from flower to flower.

14

Summer is a fun time. People like to go swimming, boating, and fishing. Many people go on vacations in the summer.

Camping is fun in the summer, too. Campfires are good for roasting hot dogs and marshmallows.

Many people enjoy picnics with family and friends. There are many parades that are fun to watch.

Spring is gone. Summer is here. Soon it will be fall.

Index

To Find Out More

Books

Fowler, Allan. *How Do You Know It's Summer?* Chicago: Children's Press, 1992.

Schweninger, Ann. *Summertime.* New York: Viking, 1992.

Webster, David. *Exploring Nature around the Year: Summer.* Englewood Cliffs, N.J.: J. Messner, 1990.

Web Sites

Athena: Earth and Space Science for K-12
http://www.athena.ivv.nasa.gov/index.html
A site dedicated to many science subjects. Includes weather topics and instructional material.

Note to Parents and Educators

Welcome to The Wonders of Reading™! These books provide text at three different levels for beginning readers to practice and strengthen their reading skills. Additionally, the use of nonfiction text provides readers the valuable opportunity to *read to learn*, not just to learn to read.

These leveled readers allow children to choose books at their level of reading confidence and performance. Level One books offer beginning readers simple language, word choice, and sentence structure as well as a word list. Level Two books feature slightly more difficult vocabulary, longer sentences, and longer total text. In the back of each Level Two book are an index and a list of books and Web sites for finding out more information. Level Three books continue to extend word choice and length of text. In the back of each Level Three book are a glossary, an index, and a list of books and Web sites for further research.

State and national standards in reading and language arts emphasize using nonfiction at all levels of reading development. The Wonders of Reading™ fill the historical void in nonfiction material for the primary grade readers with the additional benefit of a leveled text.

About the Authors

Cindy Klingel has worked as a high school English teacher and an elementary teacher. She is currently the curriculum director for a Minnesota school district. Writing children's books is another way for her to continue her passion for sharing the written word with children. Cindy Klingel is a frequent visitor to the children's section of bookstores and enjoys spending time with her many friends, family, and two daughters.

Bob Noyed started his career as a newspaper reporter. Since then, he has worked in communications and public relations for more than fourteen years for a Minnesota school district. He enjoys writing books for children and finds that it brings a different feeling of challenge and accomplishment from other writing projects. He is an avid reader who also enjoys music, theater, traveling, and spending time with his wife, son, and daughter.

Published by The Child's World®, Inc.
PO Box 326
Chanhassen, MN 55317-0326
800-599-READ
www.childsworld.com

Photo Credits
© Andy Sacks/Tony Stone Images: 13
© Bachmann/Photri, Inc.: 14
© Flanagan Publishing Services/Romie Flanagan: 9
© 1999 Mark E. Gibson/Dembinsky Photo Assoc. Inc.: 2
© 1999 Mike Barlow/Dembinsky Photo Assoc. Inc.: cover
© Myrleen Cate/Tony Stone Images: 18
© Myrleen Ferguson/PhotoEdit: 17
© 1999 NOVASTOCK/Dembinsky Photo Assoc. Inc.: 5
© Photri, Inc.: 6
© Phyllis Kedl/Unicorn Stock Photos: 21
© Terry Vine/Tony Stone Images: 10

Project Coordination: Editorial Directions, Inc.
Photo Research: Alice K. Flanagan

Library of Congress Cataloging-in-Publication Data
Klingel, Cynthia Fitterer.
Summer / by Cynthia Klingel and Robert B. Noyed.
p. cm. — (Wonder books)
Includes index.
Summary: A simple description of the summer season and its activities.
ISBN 1-56766-814-3 (lib. bdg. : alk. paper)
1. Summer—Juvenile literature.   [1. Summer.]
I. Noyed, Robert B.   II. Title.   III. Wonder books (Chanhassen, Minn.)

QB637.6 .K55   2000
508.2—dc21   99-057792